E-book: ASIN: B084BZG6DT
Paperback: ISBN: 978-1-7346042-0-7
Hardback: ISBN: 978-1-7346042-1-4
Book cover illustrated by Alyssa Kaufman
www.heliosanthosart.com

To learn more about The Fish That Drowned project, email
ANHQOL@Gmail.com
https://www.amazon.com/-/e/B084FN1F79

This book is dedicated to all the immigrants, those that have immigrant relatives, and non-profit leaders.

ACKNOWLEDGMENT

This book would not have been possible without the extra extraordinary support of many people that have to listen to the story for the last 20 plus years. It includes my wife, Dzung, my immediate family, nieces, nephews, siblings, and neighbor kids, Stephanie, Daniel, Umon & Annan. Last but not least, if it weren't for my previous coworker, Beberly Nichols Kaufman to share the story with her daughter, Alyssa Kaufman, an illustrator, this story would never published.

THE FISH
THAT

DROWNED

One day a man went to the Aquarium and
bought a goldfish.

He was so excited to take the fish home.

The man told his family….

There are two rules on how to take care the fish:
1- Never Change or add water to the tank.
2- Add some dirt to the tank every day.

As time passed, the tank's water level started getting lower and the dirt level got higher.

One day, the tank was completely dry and the fish
was comfortable living without water.

The man took the goldfish out of the tank and began showing it off to the public. They were a sensation!!!

They quickly became rich and famous.

The man and the Goldfish travel the world together! People were eager to see how a fish could learn to live without water.

A few years later, he was walking home with the goldfish on his shoulder and it started raining very hard. He took off running as fast as he could, but….

when he got home and began drying off, he realized
the goldfish was not on his shoulder anymore!

He Panicked!!!!!
He started looking for the fish everywhere!!!

He couldn't find it, so he ran outside trying to find
his beloved goldfish.

After looking everywhere, he ran to the creek
by his house…

There he saw his precious goldfish…

Floating belly-up in the creek.
The goldfish had drowned!!!

THE END

And...

THE MORAL OF THE STORY

The fish forgot who he really was...a FISH!

He forgot how to survive under water after living so many years on dry land.

It is important not to forget where you OR your family comes from, no matter what changes life may bring your way.

If we forgot the cultures, values, and principles that make us who we are today. We are at risk of becoming…

The fish that drowned!

Dear Reader,

The Fish That Drowned ideas must have come to me in around 1994 when we just moved into our new home. It probably ignited by all the reminiscent of all the traditional rituals and protocols that my parents made me do when I was a young boy. These customary rituals were ranging from long hours of the wedding ceremony of my brothers and sisters. And weeks-long preparation for the Vietnamese New Year (Tết) that I had to help out. All of these mundane activities to me at that time were like a robot. With no feeling and internally rebelling against it, because of my thoughts was, "Why we can be like an American family and do it like the American?" All of this slowly seeped and grew in me as an adult. And how I now can see why my parents made/forced me to do and be part of the above ancestral rituals. My parents want to ensure that I get to learn and hope to carry some of the "old world" pearls of wisdom, knowledge, and cultures to the new world that I'm growing in. I hope this book will help everyone to appreciate what our elders have shared and taught us. We are the bridge that connects the two worlds, "Old and New" because "What Old Is New."

Anh Doan

ABOUT THE AUTHOR

Anh Doan came from Vietnam and migrated to the U.S in 1975, settling first in Salina, Kansas and now residing in Plano, Texas since 1988. He received his Bachelor of Science in electrical engineering at Kansas State University.

Anh worked in the corporate world for 27 years and now works on his own independent insurance and financial firm.

His interest include volunteering, martial arts, and running. He is a member of One Mile for One Child non-profit organization.

Like what you read and want more of "The fish that drowned" project?

Send inquiry to ANHQOL@Gmail.com

https://www.amazon.com/-/e/B084FN1F79

ABOUT THE ILLUSTRATOR

From a young age, Alyssa Kaufman has always been ambitious and dedicated to pursuing her goals and making her dreams come true. Alyssa is a creative artist and a freelance illustrator working under the alias "Helios.Anthos."

She specializes in ink drawings and portraiture, depicting scenes exploring human sensuality and the pursuit of their higher selves. Currently, she based out of Philadelphia, PA, and can be reached at www.heliosanthosart.com.